The Hippo and the Unicorn:
A Rainbow of Words

Elaine Phillips

Cindsie Haxton

Keep
shining!

The Hippo and the Unicorn: A Rainbow of Words

Lindsie Haxton and Elaine Phillips

Illustrations by Lindsie Haxton

iUniverse, Inc.

New York Lincoln Shanghai

The Hippo and the Unicorn: A Rainbow of Words

iUniverse books may be ordered through booksellers or by contacting:

iUniverse
2021 Pine Lake Road, Suite 100
Lincoln, NE 68512
www.iuniverse.com
1-800-Authors (1-800-288-4677)

Because of the dynamic nature of the Internet, any Web addresses or links contained in this book may have changed since publication and may no longer be valid.

This is a work of fiction. All of the characters, names, incidents, organizations, and dialogue in this novel are either the products of the author's imagination or are used fictitiously.

Care has been taken to trace ownership of copyright material contained in this book. The authors will gladly receive any information that will enable them to rectify any reference or credit line in subsequent editions.

Cover design: Lindsie Haxton

ISBN: 978-0-595-43670-5 (pbk)
ISBN: 978-0-595-69490-7 (cloth)
ISBN: 978-0-595-87999-1 (ebk)

Printed in the United States of America

To

the One

Who determines

the number of the stars

and

calls each by name

Psalm 147:4

Stained glass glistening.

Heaven stooping, smiling, listening.

~ Evangeline

Reading
about
the hippo's stardust dreams
prompted the unicorn to start dreaming again.
She had once been a great believer in dreams,
but had experienced
some of the dream-breakers
her friend mentioned.

As she quietly pondered this,
it seemed as though a cloud of
iridescent-winged dragonflies
began to soar inside of her.

Could it be
that her dreams were
taking flight
again?

Thank you
to my family and friends
for believing in dreams and unicorns …

and for the beautiful way
in which each of you
colours my life.

~ Lindsie Haxton
and Evangeline

To Kateřina Srbková

Eleven years ago in Prague
you entrusted Hrošice,
the travelling hippo,
to me.

Dekuji.

~ Elaine Phillips
and Hroshi

To the Reader

Elaine Phillips and Lindsie Haxton met as classmates and discovered a synergy*
while working together on an assignment.

Upon recognizing a mutual desire to correspond, they invited Evangeline the unicorn and Hroshi the hippo to join them.

Thus two friends—no, four friends—collaborated to write an anthology of letters
that lovers of words, colours, poetry, and unexpected beauty in small things will
find delightful.

Eventually they chose to share their compilation with others. I am glad they made
that decision. In this world of war, and pain, and fractured relationships, these
vignettes help us know that there is goodness and beauty all around us.

Hroshi and Evangeline gather richness and blessing for us from that which might
otherwise pass through our lives as common and ordinary.

Barbara Wyman, PhD
Professor of Developmental Psychology and Religious Education
Cochrane, Alberta
May 2007

*The simultaneous action of separate agencies which, together, have greater total effect than
the sum of their individual parts.

PROLOGUE

Dear Reader

Are you longing for a touch of stardust in your life?

The Hippo and the Unicorn: A Rainbow of Words is a series of letters between an earthy hippopotamus, Hroshi (pronounced "Rô-she"), and an ethereal unicorn, Evangeline. In their correspondence, the writing duo contemplate life.

As co-authors of these letters, our hope is that your own sense of wonder will be renewed.

May the insights offered by the hippo and the unicorn inspire your passion for life, your curiosity, your openness to epiphanies and your ability to recognize the *extra*ordinary in the ordinary.

Elaine Phillips
and Hroshi

Lindsie Haxton
and Evangeline

P.S. You may notice that there appear to be spelling discrepancies in some of the letters. Hroshi consistently uses the **s** variant in words such as *cosy* and *realise*, while Evangeline prefers the **z** variant (a cozy alternative). Readers in North America will be more familiar with *mailboxes* and *licorice* (with a **c**) than with *postboxes* full of *liquorice* (with a **q**), the European equivalent. The hippo and unicorn originally came to live with us from two different worlds, and instead of editing out their differences, we have chosen to let them tell their stories in their own words.

PRE-STORY

"Would you write to me?"

Imaginary, or imaginative? You decide.

It all began with a phone call, late one starry night, between two friends ...

"Evangeline, dear, would you be interested in corresponding with me?" asked Hroshi the hippo.

On the other end of the telephone, in a cozy abode in Cochrane, came an immediate affirmative response from Evangeline the unicorn.

Thus, dear Reader, ***The Hippo and the Unicorn: A Rainbow of Words*** was brought into being.

Soon both correspondents were inscribing their thoughts and dreams onto writing paper, tucking the letters into multi-hued envelopes, addressing them and licking them shut, and trundling off to the post office to mail them.

Now that their first letter-anthology has been compiled, Hroshi and Evangeline invite you to lift the flap of each envelope to see what lies inside. May your hearts be coloured by their rainbow of words.

"It's something I've always dreamed of."

Once upon a dream …

> *… there lived a hippo and a unicorn*
> *who shared a simple vision of writing letters.*

Dear Evangeline

11 November, 11:11 p.m.

This evening, November the 11th, I remember reading the clock dial just before I got up—or rather down—out of my hammock. (Hippos are nocturnal creatures, as you know.)

Almost without knowing why, I knew that the date and time were right for inspiration.

I want to remember.

I want to dream.

I want to write.

For some time now I have felt inspired to share my memories and dreams and writings with a kindred spirit. Tonight my thoughts went out to you, across my room and across time and space.

Please write back to me and tell me what you enjoy doing, reading and dreaming about. I know that you enjoy *being* as much as I do.

Love,
Hroshi

Dear Hroshi

How right you are … I do enjoy being. As a matter of fact, many refer to my kind as a mystical *being*.

Thank you for the invitation to correspond with you. Yes! I would love to.

Earlier today I had pulled on my fuzzy blue mittens and scarf, zipped up my cozy coat, and with great anticipation made my way through the packed snow to the mailbox. I gently pushed open the frigid steel compartment, and despite the cold weather, an unexpected warmth filled me as I held your letter.

Your first note to me has been like a breath of spring on this frosty wintry afternoon.

I am trying to cultivate a thankful heart—and in order to do so, I started a list of things that make me happy.

Once I started my list, it was hard to stop.

Happily yours,
Evangeline

P.S. Perhaps writing to each other may fill a missing piece in both of our lives.

When I think of us
I see a hippopotamus
Who may have been a touch forlorn
Until she met a unicorn.

On the day that her first correspondence from the unicorn arrived, the letter-loving hippo could barely speak for joy.

Dear Evangeline

You are so dazzling and pure and white; you have an ageless beauty. I'm getting older and greyer (actually, I've always been grey—it's one of my two favourite colours) and I'm starting to show my age.

Twice my seams have split, requiring stitches and the silken touch of my African grandmother's healing hands. It's hard to admit that I fall apart at times! Thank you for accepting me just as I am.

Enough about externals.

My desire when writing to you is to share what's on my hippo-mind, and to engage you in the kind of conversation and correspondence that only a unique unicorn would appreciate.

I have no idea how you will respond to some of the things I share, but I ask that you remain open, and I promise to do the same.

Hippo-sized hugs on a suitably grey day,
Hroshi

P.S. Words, words, words make me happy.

Dear Hroshi

Like you, I am wild about words.

I love ...

the sound of words ...

the look of words ...

the touch of words ...

and the refreshing taste of words ...

both in my mind and in my mouth.

words
words
words
WORDS
words

To help quench your thirst for words, here is a segment from a word-wet poem which conjures up images of tumbling white waterfalls:

THE CATARACT OF LODORE
~ Robert Southey[i]

How does the water
come down at Lodore?

... Advancing and prancing and glancing and dancing,
Recoiling, turmoiling and toiling and boiling ...
....
And flapping and rapping and clapping and slapping,
And curling and whirling and purling and twirling ...
....
And so never ending, but always descending,
Sounds and motions for ever and ever are blending
All at once and all o'er, with a mighty uproar,
And this way the water comes down at Lodore.

Love,
Evangeline

P.S. "The great thing about getting older is that you don't lose all the other ages you've been."[ii]

Dear Evangeline

The poem reminds me of a **kaleidoscope** (from the Greek adjective *kalos*, meaning beautiful, and *eidos*, form or shape). A kaleidoscope of words changes shape, turning and tumbling as it creates a new pattern or image, just as in the word-waterfall.

Southey's poem decidedly places him in the category of a fellow **logophile**, or word-lover. (Is there such a word?) One of the reasons I began corresponding with you is my desire to have an audience to share the cascade of words within my hippo-soul. Sometimes I can do little to stem the tide. Thanks for joining me on my journey.

Shall we attempt a poem or two of our own?

I look forward to hearing about your happy list and shall waddle to the little grey postbox on Cochrane Lake Trail each day in anticipation of your response.

Hroshi

Hroshi

I used to enjoy writing poetry and would like to revive my poetic side. Perhaps we could rediscover the poetess within each of us.

I wish that I
Could paint the sky
With rainbow's hue
And wrap it up for you.

I hope that the rainbow thoughts I am thinking will splash onto you as you read this.

In my next letter I'll share more colourful thoughts with you; I may even compose another verse ...

Evangeline

Dear Evangeline

I can picture you painting the sky.

Your rainbow thoughts cheerfully washed over my day, and I copied your little verse onto a scrap of paper.

Hroshi

Dear grey Hroshi

I have a journal where I like to keep a record of things that make me happy. It is a juicy tangerine shade with iridian-blue lettering, a pleasure to look at and to write in.

Since my earliest memory, I have been intrigued by colours and the feelings they evoke. I cannot imagine how dull it would be to live in a newsprint-coloured world:

> Grey sky,
> grey grass,
> grey trees.

> Grey peacocks,
> grey bluebirds,
> grey geese.

> Grey pillows,
> grey sheets unfurled.

> Oh—what a wearisome world.

Colour is the language of life, and each varied hue imparts a message.

Colours are also multilingual and take on different meanings in different cultures; let's explore these nuances in the future.

Did you know that **black** is the compilation and absorption of colours of every wavelength in the spectrum? Black cloaks them in its folds, rendering them invisible to the eye.

The print in books, magazines, newspapers and on computer screens is black. Yet, paradoxically, these monochromatic letters paint words, thoughts, characters and experiences of every colour.

Black is strong, rich in depth and creativity. Whenever I wear black I sense its strength.

You mentioned in your letter that **grey**, a variant tone of black, is one of your favourites. Cross-checking my thesaurus, I saw that many of the synonyms for grey were colourless words: *characterless, cheerless, cloudy, dismal, drab, dull ...*

Certainly not descriptive of you, my colourful friend.

In the midst of such dreary words, I found *ancient*. I must agree, there is about you a timelessness, as well as an ability to view life in gradations of colour.

There is a time for seeing things in black and white and a time for shades of grey.

On you, grey shades are quite becoming.

Evangeline

Evangeline

Usually I am accused of seeing life through rose-tinted spectacles (a valid observation).

> Your allusion to grey lenses
> was a welcome change.

You surprise me; your gentle encouragement inspires me. You bring out hidden treasures in me: the distant memory of being a poet—was it long ago?—the certainty of someone reading my writing (untidy as it is) and smiling.

What is it that has opened up this well in me, this spring of life and love and laughter?

I have always been a happy hippo; my childhood was blessed. Yet recently, my life seems more—what words shall I choose to describe it?—fulfilled; contented; rich.

Ever since I began my correspondence with you, something in me began to grow. Somewhere deep down in the hidden heart of my stuffing, a writer's drumbeat could be heard, rhythmically accompanying the sound of my paws scratching on paper.

I feel an almost urgent longing to write, night and day, uninterrupted by an internal editor.

The beat continues.

Living *la vie en rose*,
Hroshi

P.S. I am thankful that you're reading what I'm writing, and smiling.

Hroshi

You are faithful to the rhythms of your soul.

Like you, I am finding words welling up within that I cannot wait to share with you.

Next on my joy-giving colour list is white. When added to colours, white softens and diffuses them, creating luminosity. (Your grey hide, a blend of black softened by white, seems to have its own inner glow.)

White is often associated with cleanliness or freshness. Picture a quiet snowfall, transforming a multicoloured world with the hushed descent of each crystalline flake.

Or a waterfall, plunging to its depths in a culmination of foam and froth.

Or a stack of fluffy white towels, freshly tumble-dried, or hung out in the sunshine and fragrant with spring breezes.

White is the colour of surrender. It is peace, safety and protection.

White is whipped cream, vanilla lattes and sugary meringues.

The appearance of white is made possible by the presence of darkness. Moonglow and stardust would not be visible without the backdrop vault of night. How beautifully Longfellow conveys this:

> "... as the evening twilight fades away,
> the sky is filled with stars, invisible by day."[iii]

White has a connotation of purity, often symbolizing holiness.

Imagine
a host of angels,
the lucent wing of a dove,
flashing bolts of lightning,
crisp linen draping an altar,
or the folds on a christening gown.

My own white colouring carries implicit expectations. When I fall short of these, the resulting failure is conspicuous. Picture me, if you will, sporting an errant drop of chocolate sauce—a light-hearted example, but I know you get the point.

Hroshi, you have always accepted me, despite the occasional spot I may sport on my pure-white coat. In my next letter I'll tell you how a recent spot came to be.

Evangeline

Dear Hroshi

I had treated myself to a sundae and chose chocolate and marshmallow toppings. Everything was fine, and I was enjoying my creamy treat, until I accidentally dripped some chocolate sauce onto my front hoof.

I must confess to you that spots bother me (although I am fond of the spots on Dalmatians and leopards and ladybugs. I like freckles, too, which are certainly a kind of spot, and as I think of it, distant stars in the night sky can look spotty too, as can the raisins in cinnamon bread. All of these are the *good* kind of spots).

But getting back to my dilemma, there it was ... a small chocolatey stain. I didn't have the heart to finish my sundae, because thoughts of the spot consumed me. Even when I covered it with a serviette, I was aware of its presence. I kept staring at it, and as I stared, it seemed to grow darker and bigger.

Finally, rousing myself to action, I found a soft cloth and some warm, soapy water, and soon:

> The spot
> was not
> a spot.

> It had
> become
> a clean, wet dot!

Now I feel sheepish (yes, there are times when a unicorn can feel like a sheep, and this was one of them).

How foolish I was to let so small a thing spoil the joy of my ice cream treat. I have decided to change my spots and, henceforth, I shall endeavour not to focus on the spots in my life.

Evangeline

Evangeline

Your snippets of poetry have inspired me to try my paw at composing an ode or two. Perhaps I should brainstorm with you.

How do *you* write poetry, Evangeline? Does it simply flow from your creative hooves? Send me some ideas, please.

Every bit of stuffing within me yearns to write ... but nothing comes out as poetry.

Hroshi

Dear Hroshi

Within the depths of your stuffing I sense a poet—*one who displays creative power or expresses beauty of thought, feelings or spirit.*

According to my reasoning, you are a poetess, Hroshi. You only have to believe!

With regards to how I write poetry:

> Sometimes
> It's simply breezy.
> And other times
> It's not so easy.
>
> Sometimes
> My thoughts flow
> And other times
> They're *verrry* slow.
>
> Sometimes
> The words rhyme,
> Like *inviting*
> And *exciting*,
> And others they don't rhyme at all.
>
> But it's all poetic writing!

I compare writing poetry to arranging flowers; wildflowers and grasses gathered into a pretty glass bottle can be as lovely to behold as a bouquet purchased from a flower shoppe. I pick whatever thoughts or words are in my mind and then use my imagination to arrange them in the right container.

Within your hippo-soul, Hroshi, there are fields of flowers awaiting the touch of your paw to harvest them.

Evangeline

P.S. I treasure seeing life through your insightful grey hippo-eyes.

Dear Evangeline

Yes, I do have to believe, and it helps to have someone who believes in me!

Hroshi

P.S. The image of the field of wildflow'rs freed me from the struggle to culti-vate a more manicured garden of words.

The unicorn couldn't fall asleep. She tossed and turned, then sleepily glanced at the clock beside her bed. A Mona Lisa smile crept over her face as she noted the time:

11:11

The magical hour.

Dear Hroshi

Maybe it was the chocolate chip cookies that I had eaten right before bed, or maybe it was the bright moonlight streaming into my room. Whatever the reason, I was wide awake.

I decided to make the most of my nocturnal alertness, and so I tip-toed quietly down the hallway to my library.

There was no doubt about it; I felt *inspired*. And I knew exactly what had inspired me:

11:11

Ever since your phone call to me that starry night, this neatly aligned, symmetrical number has had an inexplicable effect upon both of us. I tried to capture my thoughts on the matter:

ODE TO 11:11

A one and a one
and
then twice more.

How is it
that four
numbers of

comparatively
unassuming worth
have come to birth
pre-midnight flights
of fantasy?

Each *one*
points up,
yet
downward too,
like sentinels,
it would seem

reminding us that
though our feet
are tethered
to the earth

our hearts can soar.

11:11
has opened up
a door
of
enchanting
possibilities

for you
for me.

I feel a sense of satisfaction at being so completely caught up in trying to capture the essence of 11:11. It might not be a perfect poem, but I was perfectly happy writing it: an example of living in the moment.

Time, at last, for bed,
Evangeline

Dear Evangeline

We need to be wise in our choices—precisely because there are so many enchanting possibilities in life.

I seek a balance between simplicity and complexity.

However difficult it is to find the time for solitude, I know I need it. The hours alone refresh my spirit and renew my energy.

Sometimes I write … or nap … or simply dream.

I read; I ponder; I play.

Although I am gregarious, I have less to contribute to others when pouring from an empty cup.

Even in my closest friendships I embrace margin time; I am becoming a mistress of the margin.[iv]

I refuel when I spend time completely alone.

These breathing spaces fill my hippo-lungs with oxygen so that I may fully enjoy the present.

Hroshi

P.S. "But let there be spaces in your togetherness, and let the winds of the heavens dance between you."[v]

Dear Evangeline

Shall we invite our Reader to join us as we reflect on the importance of time?

Hroshi

Dear Hroshi

Yes, let's! A timely idea.

Evangeline

Dear Reader

Is there a time of day or night that is important to you? Or perhaps even a day of the week or month or year?

How does it make you feel?

What memories does it evoke?

Is there someone you know who treasures this time in a similar way?

Hroshi and Evangeline

Dear Hroshi

This week I read a poem about a hippo sandwich.

At first I expected it to be about a hippo making a sandwich. As I scanned the poem, however, I was startled to see that it was actually about a sandwich made with a hippopotamus as its key ingredient!

RECIPE FOR A HIPPOPOTAMUS SANDWICH
~ by Shel Silverstein[vi]

A hippo sandwich is easy to make. All you do is simply take
One slice of bread, One slice of cake, Some mayonnaise,
One onion ring,

One hippopotamus

One piece of string, A dash of pepper—that ought to do it.
And now comes the problem ... Biting into it!

I decided to write my own version of a hippo sandwich poem, in deference to the esteem with which I hold you and your hippo kin:

A hippo sandwich may be easy to make
But why would anyone want to take

A herd of hippopotami

And serve them in a loaf of rye?
A grave mistake!

Love,
Evangeline

Dear gracious Evangeline

I concur with your response to Shel Silverstein's hilarious poem! I found a book of his poetry at a bookshop; I'm still laughing at the ludicrous illustrations.

"And now comes the problem … Biting into it!" Can you imagine?

Hroshi

GREEN

YELLOW   BLUE

ORANGE   INDIGO

RED   VIOLET

... a rainbow of colours
and so many black words
to express them.

Hroshi

Red is a loud colour and often issues an admonition.

Red is never passive; it is passionate and pulsating.

Red is flaming sunsets.

Searing comets.

Sizzling lava.

Crackling flames.

It is scorching sunburns and scraped shins and blistering blisters.

Red is significant in life's passage and is frequently associated with beginnings and endings.

Red is loving hearts and life-saving crosses.

Dear Hroshi

Orange, a compilation of red and yellow, is an energetic colour, synonymous with joy, sunshine and warmth.

Orange is marigolds neatly lining a garden plot.

It is the folded wings of a visiting ladybug.

Orange is a meditative Monarch butterfly.

It is the sudden luscious squirt from an orange.

Orange is a cheerful school bus packed with rambunctious children.

It is soul-warming, flickering fireplace flames ...

... shared with a friend.

Dear Hroshi

Yellow is the golden eye of our solar system; the source of light and heat that preserves our lives.

Yellow is mouth-puckering lemons;
buttery, salt-sprinkled ears of corn;
softly flickering candles;
and halos curving round the heads of angels and saints.

English poet William Wordsworth captures an image of an encounter with a field of yellow flowers:

"For oft when on my couch I lie
In vacant or in pensive mood
They flash upon the inward eye
Which is the bliss of solitude
And then my heart with pleasure fills
And dances with the daffodils."[vii]

Evangeline

Hroshi

Green evokes sweet memories in me, for it was my mother's favourite colour. Although not Irish, she embraced the Celtic culture and savoured all she could about the mystical Emerald Isle. What a merry sight she was with her sparkling green eyes. (Some say I have my mother's eyes.)

Green is a smooth-sided canoe gliding over a sun-dappled lake.

It is a cascading willow.

Green is the curve of a pear ... or the briny crispness of a juicy pickle.

Green is life and hope. Green is lush and flourishing and alive.

Every year, our winter-chilled earth eagerly welcomes the first slender shoots of the prairie crocus, a harbinger of spring. This little poem sprang out of me last Easter when I spotted my first crocus:

> I delight to see the crocus
> blooming small and sweet
> 'midst morning grass.
> As I walk past,
> I stoop
> to touch
> your petals.
> Tiny thing; such joy to me you bring.

Evangeline

Hroshi

Blue is emotive.

It is oceans, rivers, lakes and streams.

It soothes.

It refreshes.

It heals.

Witnessing the ocean's surge and ebb, one can almost feel the tug of its energy upon the heart. Its blue dance fills the beholder with a primordial yearning. Do you ever long for the water of your homeland, Hroshi?

Blue is also the heavens ... the water of my homeland.

Such upward thoughts can elicit nostalgia, but I shall
choose to
refuse to
feel blue.

Evangeline

P.S. Here's an interesting detail about green and blue: green is rarely discerned in the sky, an exception being the Aurora Borealis. Conversely, blue food is not commonly found in nature.

Hroshi, dear

Indigo and **violet** are the last two rainbow colours.

Purple is synonymous with royalty.

Purple is Easter ... a time of re-creation, transition, change.

Purple is sensitive and winsome.

Have you ever witnessed a lavender sunset?

A mauve tulip?

A violet-hued rose?

A lilac-tinged egg?

All rare, and because of that, especially memorable.

Purple is ... a grape-flavoured Popsicle, dripping in the heat of a carefree day and tasting like ... a summer afternoon.

Evangeline

P.S. Purple is your other favourite colour, isn't it?

"Summer afternoon, summer afternoon,
the loveliest words in the English language."[viii]

Dear Evangeline

In my next letter, my hope is to respond to the wonder found in your colour-words. I now have almost two handfuls (paws full?) of envelopes, and I feel a bubble of glee bursting within when I open your bright correspondence box.

When I re-read the images captured in print, I find myself humming for no apparent rhyme or reason. Speaking of rhymes, I am in the process of writing a poem, inspired by your colourful letters …

Hroshi

P.S. How did you know purple was another favourite colour?

Dear Hroshi

I've noticed the soft purple of your ears. But which shade, I wonder, do you prefer ...

amethyst?
periwinkle?
purplish blue?

Purple is inspiring, and so are you.

I have a penchant for periwinkle and sing its name like a tiny tune:

Periwinkle,
Periwinkle,
Periwinkle blue.
Periwinkle,
Periwinkle,
I love you.

(sung to the tune of *Twinkle Twinkle Little Star*)

Peri means *around about, encircling, surrounding*. The root of winkle is *wink*, meaning *to shine intermittently, to twinkle*. It reminds me of your shimmering soul.

Hroshi, perhaps your deep inner soul colour is periwinkle blue.

Love,
Evangeline

P.S. Periwinkle is a plant with small flowers, often grown as a ground cover. It is also the name given to a snail with a labyrinth-like shell.

Evangeline, I'd never thought of my soul-colour before I read your letter.

Colours have diverse connotations in different cultures. In the Zulu tribe of South Africa, intricate beadwork designs send a message to the recipient. In the same way that meaning is discerned from letters strung together, so colour-combinations speak a distinct language.

Perhaps all souls have colour, Evangeline, and not only the souls of people with the gift of **synaesthesia**. An example of this phenomenon is found in the line: "I smile at the *sound* of your *touch*."[ix]

Synaesthesia occurs when a colour evokes a specific smell, or when the hearing of a certain sound induces the visualisation of a certain colour. The Hungarian composer, Franz Liszt, would apparently ask orchestra members for "a little more blue in the strings, please!"

Hroshi,
off to hunt for my African beads

P.S. Synaesthesia is *a sensation produced in one part of the body when a stimulus is applied to another.*

Dear Hroshi

How interesting to read about the Zulu beadwork. In light of this method of communication, I wonder how the colour combinations of the rainbow would be interpreted.

Although not a rainbow hue, my colour commentary wouldn't be complete without the inclusion of ... brown.

Brown is earthy and organic.

It is tree limbs and trunks.

Almonds, acorns, walnuts.

Leaves crackling underfoot.

Doe-eyed deer.

Scuffed leather shoes.

Muddy riverbanks with hippos happily wallowing.

Brown is, most emphatically ...

... Chocolate, broken into neat little squares or eaten whole.

Love,
Evangeline,

off to find some chocolate—and perhaps a friend to share it with!

Dear Evangeline

Once I dreamed my surroundings were all black-and-white—much like your description of a newsprint-coloured world—and I possessed a paintbrush containing all the colours of the rainbow on its glossy black bristles.

What fun I had in my dream turning shades of light and dark into a prism of unimaginable beauty!

Love,
Hroshi

(with a paintbrush in my left paw and a palette in my right)

Hroshi

I can only imagine what the world looked like after you had finished painting it with your palette!

Did you happen to see the rainbow the other night? Its unexpected appearance prompted me to write to you. Normally, at this time of night, I am reading under my patchwork quilt.

It (the rainbow, not the quilt) was flickering and glimmering in a grey and blustery sky—not in the least the sort of sky in which one would anticipate a rainbow. From my vantage point, it appeared to be poised right over your cozy home by the lake.

What an extraordinary sight it was; I sent a wish upon it for you.

Hroshi, you are like that rainbow in the sky—an unexpected burst of brightness in a world that can sometimes be dark and dreary.

You are radiant.

If I were a spider like Charlotte, I would weave it on a web that stretched across the heavens for the entire world to see.

People may observe your down-to-earth grey exterior and make assumptions about your nature—but if they do, they are wrong.

How erroneously we judge and are judged by our exteriors.

Evangeline

Dear Evangeline

I am going to save up my pennies in my hippo-bank and buy myself some coloured crayons, or pastel chalks, because I've always wanted to try my paw at sketching rainbow-type scenes. (Currently I cannot even draw a stick-hippo, but I may have hidden talents in the lining of my stuffing!)

I can picture you quietly reading under your patchwork quilt. This is something else we have in common.

I was enthralled by your description of the rainbow poised right over my cosy lake home:

> "flickering and glimmering / in a grey and blustery sky."

Thank you for sending a wish upon our rainbow.

I do not remember seeing it, which got me thinking:

Sometimes the loveliest scenes are right before our eyes (and in my case, under my very large nose), and yet we miss them. I shall keep an eye open for unexpected rainbows in future! It makes me happy that you saw it, dear colour-loving creature that you are.

I felt as though I saw it through your eyes via your bright words.

When you likened earthy-grey *me* to that rainbow over the lake, my eyes (most unexpectedly) filled with tears. What a kind thing to say. I see *you* as the radiant one.

Thank you for not judging me by my exterior. Here's to the beauty within us all!

Radiantly yours,
Rainbow-Hroshi

P.S. "It is not often that someone comes along who is a true friend and a good writer. Charlotte was both."[x]

Evangeline, like Charlotte, you are in a class by yourself.

Dear Evangeline

At last: here's a selection of verses from the rainbow poem you've inspired me to write.

I picked some of your images, added a few of my own, and arranged them into a bouquet:

KALEIDOSCOPE OF COLOURS

The world is ablaze with colour:
a spectrum of rainbow delight.
Red, orange and yellow will warm you;
violet-blue's the cool colour of night.

Poppies and roses are wine-red,
and sunset's the colour of blood.
African earth's ruddy and dusty;
post-drought rains turn red earth to mud.

Orange Namaqualand daisies:
an African sight to behold;
the wings of African hoepoes
flash greetings as they unfold.

Yellow is post-summer sweetcorn,
lightly buttered and sprinkled with salt;
and yellow's the taste of raw honey
with the natural colour of malt.

Green fern fronds and moss and pale seaweed,
a sapling pushing up through the sand:
each of these has its own verdant variance
from a palette of colours that's grand.

Blue is water and harbours and oceans;
it is glacial lakes and deep streams.
Blue refreshes and soothes and caresses:
the pleasant colour of dreams.

Delphiniums, irises, pansies:
blue-hued flow'rs provide merely hints
of the rainbow's remaining two colours:
a duo of glorious tints.

Indigo-ink leaves its traces on parchment:
a reminder of the power of words.
A pair of lilac-breasted rollers
flit with the freedom of birds.

Violets dappled with dew in the morning
lift their faces with joy to the world.
At the sight of their velvety petals,
a tender response is unfurled ...

Mystical, magical, winsome:
purple's a colour both royal and rare.
It is tulips and roses and mauve-tinted eggs
of which we are seldom aware.

From red through to violet we've travelled,
exploring our colour-rich earth.
Scattered around us you'll find them:
infinite treasures of worth.

~ Hroshi

Hroshi

Your recent responses revealed further talents hidden beneath your humble grey exterior.

You are like a museum, housed in ancient stone. Inside are myriads of corridors leading to diverse exhibits of imagination and curiosity: our friendship is the entrance ticket for me to walk through those hallways and chambers.

Life has become more fascinating with you as my friend and you have taught me much, just by being you ... an astute and happy-hearted hippo.

Evangeline

Dear sunny Evangeline

After last week's rain the sun has reappeared to warm the wintry earth.

While you love being out in the open air and in the sun, I'm a water-lover.

Perhaps you can share my joy when it rains. For unfathomable reasons, I simply love rain.

I love walking in the rain, singing in the rain, swimming in the rain (although I get more wet than usual), and watching rain as it dances on the windowpane.

Hroshi

P.S. Life here on Cochrane Lake is glorious for a water-loving hippo, although the lake will soon freeze over for the winter.

Dear Hroshi

It must be wondrous living by a lake. What do you see when you look out your window?

When I gaze out of mine, there are many trees, one of which is especially charming.

Trees remind me of people: they have roots, trunks and limbs; they change their clothing with the seasons; and they have personalities.

My window-tree has daintily dropped her golden leaves around her toes, leaving each branch bare. Now I am able to see the flutter of even the tiniest visiting bird and the occasional lingering leaf. With her foliage gone, the blue comes through.

My tree has also privileged me with a glimpse of her heart, as witnessed one recent evening when the glowing, rosy-red sun rested deep within her boughs.

The tree is transparent with me, and she is teaching me much ...

> ... about herself and others.

Love,
Evangeline

P.S. As I watched from my window today, it unexpectedly began to snow. What an unpredictable climate we live in!

Hroshi

Today the snow continues to fall and I wrap my cozy quilt more snugly around me. Maybe it is this stay-inside cold weather that is causing me to contemplate.

As I watch through the window, the silence of the snow strikes me anew. Even though it doesn't make a sound, I hear it speaking.

Typically it comes without fanfare (unless, of course, there is a tremendous blizzard), and then ...

> quietly,
>
> peacefully,
>
> calmly ...
>
> it snows.

In pensive mood,
Evangeline

P.S. Reading Wordsworth's lyrical poem about daffodils has inspired me to write one of my own.

THE SNOWFLAKES

I pondered at my windowpane,
not quite asleep,
not quite awake,
when all at once I saw a throng ...
a host of many a snowy flake
descending from cerulean skies,

dancing and twirling
before my eyes.

The earth that morn was hushed;
it turned its rosy face to view their flight.
They danced by dawn and afternoon;
they danced into the amber night.
I gazed enrapt,
wholly in awe
of what I felt and all I saw.

And now,
reclining on my bed
in pensive and reflective frame,
their chorus rings within my head,
resplendent ...
like angelic flame.
My heart is stirred,
uplifts,
awakes,
and dances with the snowy flakes.

     ~ Evangeline

Thank you for sharing your snowflake poem, Evangeline. As I read it I found myself gazing at the garden which has changed its garments overnight.

What *do* I see when I look out my window?

A forest of trees (not of green, today, but with their bare branches lifted up to the heavens). The fresh snow certainly adds beauty to the browns of winter.

Your tree is transparent with you: I like that in a tree. We have much to learn from our friends in nature.

Today, as I look out my window at our white garden, the Christmas tree, a strand of lights recently entwined around its branches, glows invitingly.

You must come and see it for yourself.

Hroshi

P.S.
"My heart is stirred,
uplifts,
awakes,
and dances with the snowy flakes."

The unicorn closed her eyes and imagined the lights glowing on her friend's Christmas tree.

Hroshi

I sense so many colours within you, my outwardly grey friend:

> bright and bold colours;
> soft and sensitive colours.

Have you ever considered that hearts can be like prisms? When the sun shines into a prism, it strikes the facets of crystal and reveals the colours hidden inside.

Our world can be dark, not only in the winter, and I am thankful that the sun shines into your heart, refracting rainbows into the lives of others.

Evangeline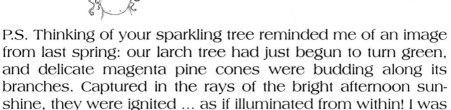

P.S. Thinking of your sparkling tree reminded me of an image from last spring: our larch tree had just begun to turn green, and delicate magenta pine cones were budding along its branches. Captured in the rays of the bright afternoon sunshine, they were ignited ... as if illuminated from within! I was spellbound.

As a water-loving hippo do you mind this winter weather?

Dear Evangeline

I do not dislike the cold, and I find the snow breathtakingly beautiful, but the wind makes my ears ache. You see, I'm used to the snow since much of my early childhood was spent in the Czech Republic (with a European climate similar to Canada's) before I returned to Africa for a few years.

But oh, the wind! My marrow-stuffing shivers at the thought.

I think the frozen lake is lovely, especially when the neighbourhood children skate on its icy surface. Shall I learn how to skate in the winter, I wonder, until I can swim again in the spring?

Once in a while, I hop in the bathtub or shower—although, I admit, it's a trifle small and I find the turning of the taps a bit awkward.

As I sit here and write, darkness is closing in, but my soul shimmers with the sunshine of your letter.

I can imagine you in your blue mittens and scarf making your way through the packed snow to the postbox. What a pretty picture.

I smile as the image expands to include a purple envelope being dropped lovingly into the mail slot by way of response. Thanks for your swift reply.

I shall make the short trip to the curve in the road every day next week while I await your next letter.

My paws are clumsy on this cold night, and there is much to share, but I sense you are a patient reader. One day soon I will write and tell you how I felt upon opening your envelope. Since I wish to post this in the morn, I'll end now and write more on the morrow.

 Hroshi

P.S. Evangeline, dear, your name is rather poetic. We've known each other for a while now, and yet I realise I don't know whether or not you have a second name. Do you?

Yes, I do have a second name. I didn't realize that you didn't know.

I'll give you a clue: it starts with J.

Can you guess what it is?

Love,
Evangeline J

Dear Evangeline J

J for Jane?

Jeru*salem*? (Did you know that *salem* means peace?)

Jewel? (You certainly are a gem to me, and you bring a sense of peace wherever you go.)

Be sure to tell me in your very next letter.

Curious,
Hroshi

P.S. My full name—Hrošice, pronounced "Rô-she-tsê"—means *girl hippo* in the Czech language, but Hroshi is easier to spell.

Dear Hroshi

My father
named me Evangeline,
which means
messenger of good news;

and Joy,
because
he *rejoiced* at my birth.

With Joy,
Evangeline

P.S. I'm looking forward to the day you meet my sisters, Angelica and Gloria.

Angelica   Gloria[xi]

Dear Evangeline Joy

Three unicorns! Magnificent. I look forward to meeting your sisters.

It's difficult for you to be confined inside since you love to soar. I can imagine you up, up in the clouds, high above the waters of the lake and the grasses of the field near our home. Nevertheless, you are cultivating a thankful heart. Gratitude is an admirable quality.

Your idea of keeping a happy list has inspired me. Since reading your first letter, I have been saving up happy things to tell you. In fact, I have begun my very own Journal of Joy. I'm in the process of transferring the notes from my countless scraps of paper into my new journal.

How I rejoice in the unexpectedness (is there such a word?) of our kindred friendship. How I value your correspondence, but far beyond the letters, I admire your character. You are my joy-sharer, my fellow word-lover.

You don't scoff at my BIG ideas, nor do you belittle my tiniest adventures.

Please continue to share your journal entries with me, and I shall certainly do the same.

I understood when you said that once you'd started making a list, it was hard to stop; it reminds me of a song I like to sing: "Count your blessings, name them one by one …"

Hroshi

P.S. One of my blessings takes the shape of a very small bird-friend. Her name is Beak, and her feathery warmth is cosy on cold nights in winter.

Dear Hroshi

Will you please sing that song for me? Considering your size, I can only imagine that you must be an alto!

I, too, have a bird friend: Dahling, an aptly named elegant ostrich, who is of larger proportions than your little Beak.

Recently I read:

> "The language of birds is very ancient,
> and, like other ancient modes of speech,
> very elliptical: little is said,
> but much is meant and understood."[xii]

Dahling is such a bird with such a language.

Aren't we fortunate that these feathery creatures have roosted in our lives?

Love,
Evangeline

P.S. Here is a drawing of Dahling.

Dear Evangeline

Dahling is a beautiful bird, and the pencil sketch you sent is charming. (I did not know you could draw.) Beak and I both look forward to meeting her.

Love,
Hroshi and Beak

P.S. Evangeline, I so admire your artwork, as does little Beak. She encouraged me to try my paw at it too.

What do you think of my stick-hippo family?

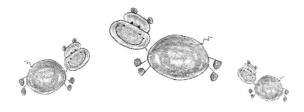

Dear Hroshi

What can I say?

Speechless,
Evangeline

P.S. Hroshi, your question places me in a rather sticky situation!

Dear Evangeline

Your silence spoke volumes.

Perhaps I should stick to writing letters rather than drawing stick figures.

Hroshi

Oh, would you really give up so easily, Hroshi?

Stick to it ...

Evangeline

Dear Evangeline

Did you mean easel-ly? I'll keep drawing stick-hippos, then.

Now, tell me more about Dahling, please.

Does she eat stones?

Does she like books?

Does she sing?

Are these questions ridiculous?

Hroshi

No, Hroshi,
your questions aren't ridiculous at all.

This blue sphere we inhabit has much to reveal, so it is good to seek and ask.

"I wrestle with nature long enough for her to tell me her secret."[xiii]

I'm happy that you are interested in learning more about Dahling. Initially, I was drawn to her by her cheerfulness, despite her inability to fly. She spent the first years of her life in captivity and it is heart-warming to watch her enjoying her new freedom.

Dahling is more inclined towards pink peppermints than stones.

She is well-read: I believe the proper term is erudite (refuting the term bird brain).

All in all, Dahling is a rather unorthodox ostrich.

I hope the two of us can meet each other's feathered friends someday soon.

Evangeline

P.S. Please tell me more about Beak.

A new day, a new week, a new month—a new idea. The hippo smiled as she thought of all she had been saving up to tell the unicorn. What an inspiration her winged kindred spirit was to her.

Dear Evangeline

A new Journal of Joy entry pertains to my love of quotes. Thank you for the Van Gogh addition. Perhaps I'll start collecting colourful quotations in the front of my journal. (I'm a left-pawed hippo and so I write back to front.)

Hroshi

P.S. Beak flew into my life on a bright Wednesday morning several Februaries ago. She has been a faithful writing companion since we met, and over time we have discovered many common interests.

Her skill with ink and quill far exceeds my own, and recently she agreed to become my personal scribe. Most of the time I pen my own letters to friends and relatives—and to you, dear Evangeline—but on occasion a lighter touch is required than my clumsy paws afford. I dictate my ideas to her and she hastily scribbles them down.

Like Dahling, Beak loves books, but more because she loves any form of paper and ink.

Beak is neat and tidy, whereas I tend to live in creative chaos much of the time. My stomping grounds are also far larger than hers.

Her nesting instincts amuse me; she collects all manner of items for her home, including feathers, chocolate eggs, and even golf balls! Remember the Zulu bead jewellery I mentioned earlier? Guess where I found it!

Currently she is cosily perched on a woolly winter toque belonging to a friend.

One of the characteristics I most admire about my cheery companion is her ability to sing even when everything seems dark and gloomy. She is truly a chirpy little soul.

Oh, Evangeline!

Here's a noteworthy thought:

When Dahling and Beak meet, we can harmonise.

Beak sings soprano—Dahling can carry the melody.

Would you accompany us on your horn?

Hroshi

Dear Hroshi

I'll polish up my horn and start practising at once; when we get together to harmonize I'll be ready.

Evangeline

Dear Hroshi

Your own personal scribe! I learn something new about you in every letter. Beak, with her curious ways, must keep you on your hippo-toes.

Thinking of that makes me imagine you as a ballerina!

Do you like to dance, Hroshi?

Evangeline

Yes, Evangeline, I do.

I dance in the moonlight, down on the riverbank (although onlookers may think I am mud-wallowing).

I dance in the midst of winter to get my blood circulation going.

I dance in the rain, usually without an umbrella, and I dance when I feel care-free on lazy summer afternoons.

I dance when I open my music box and pretend to be twirling on the blue velvet inside.

Pirouetting,
Hroshi

P.S. I dance every April on my birthday!

Dear Hroshi

Sometimes I wonder if there is some Lippizan in me. Reading about you dancing made me want to dance too. (Lippizaners are powerful white horses, famous for their "airs above the ground," which are movements much like dances.)

You dance to your own drumbeat, Hroshi. What a beautiful way to live life!

And speaking of beautiful, recently a mutual friend wrote to me with an interesting request: what was my favourite beautiful word.[xiv]

That's precisely the kind of question that appeals to me, and after some reflection I wrote back, suggesting the word madrigal.

When I was younger, my lovely literary mother[xv] taught me a poem entitled *The Ballad of Beautiful Words*, and madrigal is in line four.

Some words sound beautiful and others have a beautiful connotation: madrigal fits both categories. (Do you know what it means, Hroshi?)

Your letters to me are filled with beautiful words. As I read through them again today, I drank some of the words in so quickly that they singed my tongue.

Then I re-read them. The pale winter sunshine sifted softly through my frosty windowpane. I leaned cozily against my puffy pillows and basked in the warmth of your words.

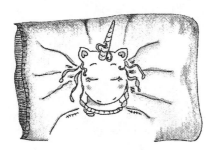

Then I read them once more as I sipped café au lait from my snowflake mug.

Words are magical, aren't they?

Your words today were like a comforting drink of hot chocolate with whipped cream on top—and a warm chocolate chip cookie.

Mmmm. Beautiful words indeed.

Evangeline

P.S. I hope that you enjoy the accompanying *Ballad*. Do you have a favourite beautiful word?

THE BALLAD OF BEAUTIFUL WORDS
~ John McCutcheon[xvi]

Amethyst, airy, drifting, dell,
Oriole, lark, alone,
Columbine, kestrel, temple, bell,
Madrigal, calm, condone.

Emerald, swallow, tawny, dawn,
Silvery, starling, lane,
Radiance, rosary, garland, fawn,
Pastoral, valley, vane.

Smouldering, sombre, tumbrel, tomb,
Indigo, ember, shorn,
Sonorous, sorrow, cloven, doom,
Pendulum, dirge, forlorn.

Charity, gloaming, garnering, grain,
Curfew, candle, loam,
Benison, mother, lassie, swain,
Children, evening, home.

Dear Evangeline

Thank you for sharing the beautiful *Ballad*. In response to your question about favourite words, I shall take some time to compile a list. (See my next letter.)

Since music brings me joy—especially on snowy, housebound evenings—the first word I thought of was orchestra: full of musical promise, wouldn't you agree?

When I read your description of a breath of spring on a frosty wintry day, I realised I felt the same about your words. It has been so bitterly cold out here of late; the wind howls around the house and down the chimney flue at night; the wooden beams creak eerily; and if I am the only soul awake in the wee hours, I go and crawl into my cosy hammock.

Hroshi

P.S. You have a way with words, do you know that?

Dear Hroshi

Yesterday I dressed in black, from my horn to my hooves.

As I trudged across a vast sunlit field of white snow, I imagined how visible I must have looked to the eagle soaring overhead, had it chosen that moment to gaze downward.

Although I felt small and seemingly insignificant,
I sensed that I was being watched over.

What a comforting feeling.

Love,
Evangeline

Evangeline

In my last letter I said I would spend some time reflecting on your question regarding a favourite beautiful word. Your choice of madrigal is pretty, isn't it? It conjures up mysterious images of sun and song … in a symbolically beautiful manner.

I looked up the word, thinking it referred to a small bird, like a sweet-voiced nightingale or lark.

Instead, I found the following definition:

> **madrigal** (**mad**-ri-gal), *noun*
> a part-song for voices, usually without instrumental accompaniment.

You already knew this, but today I learned the meaning of a new word.

Here are the first entries on my own list: serendipity, luminous and squirrel.

And I *really* like the **euphony** of the noun unicorn!

Hroshi-the-word-lover

P.S. Euphony means *having a pleasing sound*.

Dear Hroshi

The word hippopotamus has a nice weighty feel to it, too.

How serendipitous that one of your favourite words is squirrel. This winter, as I wandered by the creek near my home, I noticed many squirrels flying through the treetops.

Poor things, I thought. Are they cold? Are they hungry?

In order to ease my unease, I stuffed my pockets with peanuts-in-the-shell and placed them in hiding spots for the squirrels to discover. I knew where their nests were, so I placed the nuts where the squirrels were bound to find them.

There I was: a large being (compared to the squirrels), observing those small, industrious creatures and happily hiding little morsels for them to discover.

Bit by bit, a most delicious thought came to me.

Could it be that someone was hiding morsels for me to discover on my pathway—and deriving pleasure from my delight?

Evangeline

Skittles! As the hippo savoured first the purple-grape flavour, then a lime-green candy, she thought of how sweet the unicorn was to send her a taste of summer on a winter's day. Gratefully she reached for another fruit-full Skittle.

Dear Evangeline

In the midst of the unfriendly temperatures we've been experiencing, a taste of the tropics came to Cochrane's frozen lake district. (Speaking of things tropical, I do enjoy a sweet, juicy watermelon every so often—a tasty snack between helpings of river grass.)

You sent me a gift, you angel! What a splendid surprise. I opened the envelope with its enclosed matching sky-blue paper, not expecting to find a delicious mini-orchard of Skittles inside: berries, and grapes, and citrus fruit. For *me*.

It is rare to find a neatly wrapped present waiting in the postbox. My dear bear-friend, Camelot[xvii] (who lives across the Pond on a muddy little island), sent me some Terry's Orange chocolates for my birthday last year.

It brings me great joy to receive a gift of my very own in the mail. One memorable surprise was a box of Smarties wrapped in a pair of socks.

The vision of you trudging across a vast field of sunlit snow, dressed in black from your horn to your hooves, is a striking one. If I were a bird flying overhead, I would have swooped down to greet you, to tell you how marvellous you looked, to enjoy your simple white-and-black beauty.

No matter how small or insignificant we may *feel*, we know we are being watched over, don't we?

A comforting feeling indeed.

Hroshi

Dear Evangeline

After I showed Beak your colourful letters, she decided to compose her own little ditty in my honour. How blessed I am to count two poets among my close friends!

RAINBOW SLIDING

violet, indigo:
your purple edges add a royal touch to all my days

blue, green, yellow:
cool water, river grass, sunshine rays

orange:
the colour of the setting sun
o'er Cochrane Lake when day is done

red:
beneath the stuffing of your hippo-soul
a thread weaves together what needs to be whole

a **rainbow** of laughter;
a prism of joy:
how brightly glows the heart of no mere toy!

~ Beak (Hroshi's scribe)

Isn't she sweet?

I am sending you part of a poem about a hippopotamus. I do hope you like it. I have memorised it and gleefully recite it to friends. Let me know what you think.

Hroshi

I HAD A HIPPOPOTAMUS
~ Patrick Barrington[xviii]

I had a hippopotamus; I kept him in a shed
And fed him upon vitamins and vegetable bread.
I made him my companion on many cheery walks
And had his portrait done by a celebrity in chalks.

I had a hippopotamus; I loved him as a friend
But beautiful relationships are bound to have an end.
Time takes, alas! our joys from us and robs us of our blisses;
My hippopotamus turned out to be a hippopotamissus.

Thank you for the hippo poem,
dear Hroshi.

I read it out loud while sipping hot apple cider and now I'm
inspired to try inventing my own hippopotawords.

Evangeline

I'm glad you liked the hippo poem, Evangeline.

See if you have a flash of inspiration, and let me know.

Hroshi

Dear Hroshi

What do you think?

My housekeeper regarded her with a maternal eye,
And eagerly awaited the baby hippopotami.
She purchased massive skeins of yarn from the craft store
Snooties,
And spent all her spare time knitting hippopotabooties.

My house now resounds with hippopotanoises,
And strewn in every corner are hippopotatoyses.
The fridge and cupboard are both crammed with
hippopotafoodies.
And my housekeeper is knitting bigger hippopotabooties.

I have a hippopotamus and nothing on this earth
Could give such love and happiness and everlasting mirth.
The pleasure that she gives me is unlike any other
And I'm so glad that she became a hippopotamother.

Hippopotahappily,
Evangeline

Evangeline, you're a natural!

I laughed until my hippo-sides ached when I read your version. (I do believe the original author would have approved.)

If you keep this up, we may have to start our own hippo and unicorn anthology.

Hroshi

Hroshi

A hippo and unicorn anthology is something to dream about!

I have found a song to send you about unicorns.[xix] In it, Noah is herding all the animals onto the ark, but unfortunately the unicorns were hiding and so they didn't get on board.

The song ends:

"Then the ark started movin', and it drifted with the tide,
and the unicorns looked up from the rock and cried.
And the water came up and sort of floated them away—
that's why you've never seen a unicorn to this day."

Fortunately, Shel Silverstein wasn't accurate.

There are many today, including you, who *have* seen unicorns ... those with patient, gentle and open hearts.

"Well, now that we have found each other," said the unicorn, "If you believe in me, I'll believe in you."[xx]

Evangeline

The Lewis Carroll quote you shared brought to mind a snippet of verse from my hippo-childhood about "the possibility of being"; here's an excerpt:

> This is the creature there has never been.
> They never knew it, and yet, none the less,
> they loved the way it moved, its suppleness,
> its neck, its very gaze, mild and serene.
>
> Not there, because they loved it, it behaved
> as though it were. They always left some space.
>
> And in that clear unpeopled space they saved
> it lightly reared its head, with scarce a trace
> of not being there.
>
> They fed it, not with corn,
> but only with the possibility
> of being.
>
> And that was able to confer
> such strength, its brow put forth a horn.
> One horn.[xxi]

Evangeline, it is a rare gift to believe—and I'm thankful that you do.

Our friendship has positive consequences: you have fuelled my imagination.

I believe in possibilities as yet unexplored.

I see potential in places I'd never looked before.

Hroshi

P.S. Beak and I are looking forward to your visit immensely. We must take a photo of ourselves for my little friendship album. Let's sit in front of the fire and drink cocoa and eat animal crackers. Maybe you could teach me the tune to your unicorn song.

"Animal crackers and cocoa to drink,
That is the finest of suppers, I think;
When I'm grown up and can have what I please
I think I shall always insist upon these."[xxii]

Dear Hroshi

I can't wait to visit with you.

Evangeline Joy

Dear Evangeline

Thank you for visiting us on Monday night. You're so brave to come out on a crisp evening. As you know, you're always welcome to stay; you have your very own pink-and-blue-and-white guest pillow on which to sleep.

I do hope the self-timer photos we took come out well.

Oh! I remember the miniature white marshmallows in our cocoa—I'm so glad you share my sweet tooth.

Hroshi

Dear Evangeline

Chasing rainbows: don't these two words conjure up a colourful image?

Yesterday's beautiful sight inspired me to stop at home long enough to grab a camera and go chasing rainbows. Thank you for joining me at such short notice.

Through the snowy park we followed the elusive band of colour across several wooden bridges.

We saw it in the distance, above the tree-line, but each time we rounded a corner it seemed to have moved or faded.

Still we wandered in the general direction of the bow, listening to the trickle of the stream beneath the ice and the evocative sounds of migrating birds.

Even now as I sit here I can smell the damp pine needles.

While out in the woods chasing rainbows with you, the gladness simmering below the consciousness of my stuffing had time to surface.

Refreshed,
Hroshi

Dear rainbow-chasing Hroshi

What a lovely rainbow photograph you sent me. I have put it on the windowsill of my sunroom to remind me of the pleasure we had traipsing through the cedar-scented woods.

If I could ever catch a rainbow, I would love to slide down its inviting upside-down smile: but they are strangely elusive.

Perhaps, like us, others are looking for some hidden rainbow.

After I got home, I put on my fuzzy slippers and pyjamas, and mused over our woodland exploration.

Rainbows are captivating, no doubt because of their alluring array of colours.

Another appealing element is their inviting arched shape ... like a curved portal, welcoming all who draw near to enter.

Would we, or other rainbow followers, be so inclined to cross its threshold if it were not a bow shape?

I think not.

The maker of the rainbow created it in such a way that it appears as though two arms are curving from the firmament, stooping down to embrace all rainbow chasers.

It's interesting that the word **bow** when pronounced *bough*, means *to bend over* or *stoop down*.[xxiii]

Snug in a heavenly hug,
Evangeline

Dear Hroshi

It is 12 noon, on the dot, a time not unlike the fulcrum of a teeter-totter. I sit balanced at this pivotal time of day in anticipation of the ups and downs that it will bring.

Up—to catch glimpses of heaven.

Down—to connect with humanity.

Up and down.

I feel the air brush past as I rise and fall with the rhythms of the day. I wish that you were on the other end of the see-saw with me and I take delight in imagining you here.

Where are you now, as I write, I wonder ...

Up?

Down?

Sitting on the fulcrum, quietly waiting?

You cannot envision my excitement when a cascade of pretty envelopes appeared on my living room table, like scattered rose petals

Which one should I open first?

In anticipation,
Evangeline

Balance. The unicorn mentioned the ups and downs of her day and the hippo began to ponder the events of her own daily life.

Dear Evangeline

As I re-read your letter (which arrived most unexpectedly in a make-my-day moment), I am entranced by the image of the teeter-totter and the fulcrum.

Up and down.

My hope is that we will catch glimpses of heaven each new day.

You write: *I feel the air brush past as I rise and fall with the rhythms of the day. I wish that you were on the other end of the see-saw with me and I take delight in imagining you here.* Let's go to a park and find a see-saw someday soon, and turn your imagining into a mutual memory.

Love,
Hroshi
(alone on the see-saw, waiting for you)

P.S. I appreciated your description, a few days ago, of this lovely blue sphere we inhabit—did your choice of writing paper match your mood?

Dear Hroshi

I wrote to you on the sky-blue paper because it reminds me to lift my thoughts upward. I wanted you to catch a glimpse of heaven with me.

Sometimes riding the teeter-totter of life comes with thuds and bumps, and looking up gives me the courage to get up again and keep on going.

I am happy that you are enjoying your own Joy Journal.

Often the little things are joy-givers: I want to remember to keep my eyes and ears and heart open so I won't miss them.

Evangeline Joy

P.S. What brings joy to you?

The unicorn asked what brought joy and the hippo began to count her blessings. Joy-givers. The hippo knew several furry-folk (and the human kind) who brought joy to others. All day long, she thought of the many small things that brought her joy:

personal correspondence from the unicorn;

a colourful gift in a bright envelope;

meeting a kindred spirit unexpectedly;

a moment of shared humour—or shared sorrow;

the breathtaking beauty of nature;

the shimmer of Northern Lights on a winter-cold night;

a fleeting glimpse of heaven.

Dear Evangeline

Today I shall tell you what brings me joy. Be prepared for several letters. Here's the first:

Life fills me with joy. Being *alive* to the goodness of each new day is a gift. I know that I am fearfully and wonderfully made.

In keeping with my love of life, I celebrate birthdays with enthusiasm, and I know you do, too.

Let's plan a combined celebration next year.

Perhaps we could start a diary that we write in as we celebrate each birthday.

In fact, birthdays make up a separate entry in my own Journal of Joy. Writing this down has started me thinking about the beauty of life in general, and the wonder of each passing year.

Philosophically,
Hroshi

P.S. Watch this space for more joy-givers.

The unicorn smiled as she read the hippo's first letter on joy-givers. "It seems to be joy-giving," thought the unicorn, "just thinking of the things that give us joy!"

Dear Hroshi

Being alive to life, as you are, is a valuable gift. You are perceptive to the many potential joy-givers in your daily life, and you have become one of *my* favourite joy-givers.

There is no doubt in my mind that if your life were measured, it would be extraordinarily large (as befitting a hippo of such girth).

Evangeline

P.S. Life is measured by the number of things that you are alive to.[xxiv]

Dear Evangeline

Upon waking up this morning, I immediately began to think of what to say in this new letter. My pond overflows with many blessings, some of which I took for granted until your recent question broke through my complacency.

Living with my extended furry family brings me joy. Each new day holds the promise of the unknown.

Friends are joy-givers, too. *You* fill my heart with cheer, Evangeline Joy.

Receiving and sending personal mail remains high on my list. Your letters provide a pool of strength, encouragement and sweetness.

Appreciation for my friends and relations flows through my hippo-veins on this rainy winter's day.

Hroshi

Dear Hroshi

I share your sentiments about the joy that loved ones bring.

I love listening to the voices of my family and friends as they are talking or laughing together. Is there anything quite as heart-warming as the sound of a voice that is dear?

Now and then I can even hear, deep inside of me, the voices of loved ones who are no longer here, and that brings me joy too.

Sometimes, if I am walking late at night, I like to glance into the brightly-lit front rooms of neighbouring homes. Illuminated inside I might see parents, children, grandparents, pets and family-related activities.

I am happy to have a place to call home ... to have my own bright room to walk into and to be part of a loving family.

Evangeline

Ah, Evangeline

We have written of special days and special friends—and now at last I come to the joy of food.

On a warm but windy Wednesday last summer you suggested that we treat ourselves to a couple of sugar cones. Vanilla was my choice and yours was maple walnut.

Down to the river we went for an afternoon of simple pleasures: a frozen feast, cosy sunshine and heart-to-heart sharing.

I will always remember our ice cream day.

Years ago I met a dear old man who told me how grateful he was for his taste buds. I hadn't thought about giving thanks for the ability to distinguish between salty, bitter, sweet and sour flavours before.

Hippos need vast quantities of nourishment to fuel them, and I'm no exception:

Edible joy-givers include fruit (my lifelong favourite being watermelon) and the kind of fruit-flavoured treats you recently sent me in the mail.

I have a special fondness for *all* citrus fruit (somewhat unusual in hippos), as well as mangoes, peaches, plums and grapes.

And who can resist strawberries with whipped cream? Since moving to Canada, I have discovered the many delights of berries: blueberries, cranberries, Saskatoon berries.

In season I may nibble on more exotic finds such as pomegranates, paw paws (similar to papinos, but larger), guavas and kiwi fruit.

However, staple items in the daily planning of hippo-meals include the more common (but no less delicious) apples and bananas available year-round.

Either fresh or dried fruit is fine. In Africa I learned to appreciate dried mango and pineapple chunks, while dried banana chips were a delicacy on the streets of Prague. And raisins by the mouthful are always welcome, in any venue.

The last time a friend brought me a whole watermelon to devour, I remember being profoundly contented; it truly is the sweetest snack.

Currently snow covers the trees in the garden outside my window, and I close my eyes and imagine the citrus-scented orchards and autumn-hued vineyards of Africa.

Hroshi

P.S. I eat veggies, too, in case you're wondering. (Hippos are herbivores and will eat almost anything green.) My soup-loving friend cooks a fabulous puréed concoction comprising five zucchinis in a blender, to which she adds carrots and onions and red, yellow and green peppers.

Dear Hroshi

With your talent and tastes you should be writing menus for restaurants.

Your letter was tantalizing, and before I was even halfway through it, I was compelled to look for something tasty to eat.

I settled for warm,
lightly salted and buttered popcorn
served in a smoothly carved wooden bowl,
with an additional sprinkling of Parmesan on top.

Along with this,
I nibbled on a thin wedge of carefully aged,
sharp, cold pack cheddar cheese.

And to top it all off,
a tall cold glass of frothy banana milk.

Contented,
Evangeline

P.S. The image of you with your sweet snack made me think: next time we visit, let's have a watermelon seed-spitting contest.

Dear Evangeline

This next topic deserves a letter of its own:

I am passionate about any and every form of chocolate.

Hot chocolate, cold chocolate and anything in between is acceptable. When finances allow the luxury, I admit I am partial to purchasing European chocolate. Whilst in Prague, I had access to a variety of inexpensive Swiss chocolates—among the finest in the world. Belgium chocolate is known for its quality, too.

Hroshi

P.S. And, oh! I am incredibly fond of liquorice. During my last visit to England, my travelling companion took a photo of me in an old-fashioned sweet shoppe in Bath.

I have also sampled Swedish confectionery. My favourite is a small black rectangle with the consistency of soft toffee and the taste of liquorice.

The unicorn's mouth watered as she read about the hippo's affection for chocolate and other delicacies. Nodding her head, she concurred with her friend's appraisal.

Dear Hroshi

Your detailed description of chocolate resonated within me. It deserves a book of its own to chronicle its surpassing merit. While on this sweet subject, I wonder if you are a bite-and-swallow chocolate eater, or a melt-in-your-mouth and savour-each-morsel aficionado.

Licorice is a favourite of mine too.

Licorice!
    Black!
        Red!
           Candy-coated!
               Cigar-shaped!

I especially enjoy the licorice candies that resemble small pink, orange or brown sandwiches with black licorice filling. These, however, must be fresh and ever so slightly *squish*able.

Evangeline

P.S. Let's see if we can discover a Canadian counterpart for your delicious Swedish confectionery.

I'm off to bed now ... sweet dreams.

Dear Hroshi

Tonight I couldn't fall asleep;
my bedcovers were in a heap.
I tossed and turned in my cozy bed
as visions of food fondly danced in my head.

My tummy rumbled and tumbled and turned;
for the feast we'd described in our letters I yearned.

Unravelling a mountain of blankets and sheets
I stumbled and grumbled and got out of bed.
"This will never do," I drowsily said.
Down the hall to the kitchen my footsteps led.

Bleary-eyed I examined the cupboard and fridge.
All the essential ingredients were there
to whip up a batch of crispy French toast
and end my midnight hour of despair.

After much measuring
and flour-sifting
and egg-breaking
and batter-whipping
and oil-tipping
and mess-making
and bread-dipping
and French toast-baking ...

my late night treat
was ready to eat.

I positioned two ovals of gold on my plate,
fairy-dusted with sugar, 'though the hour was late.
Then I added a pat of butter—just one,
and a drizzling of syrup—just for fun.

Exquisite,
extraordinary,
raspberry sweet ...

What a perfect
midnight treat!

~ Evangeline

Dear Evangeline

Thank you for your kind responses to my joy-related letters—and for the delicious description of your midnight snack. We never seem to run out of joy-givers, do we?

Here are today's entries:

I enjoy going for a midnight swim or a moonlit stroll along the banks of Cochrane Lake.

Devouring large quantities of my daily staple, river grass, brings its own fulfilment.

On the weather-front, I like rain (in all its forms of precipitation).

Snow fascinates me; I can watch it for hours. I would like to learn how to ski.

Isn't it amazing to think that no two snowflakes are the same? Each tiny feather of frozen glass has its very own fingerprint.

While I do enjoy walking in the snow once in a while, I prefer being bundled up inside, beside the fire ... which brings me to another joy-giver:

Fire. How I love the cosy ambience created by the glow of candlelight, or the comforting sound of a crackling hearth-fire. I even enjoy the crisp scratch of a match being lit. Let's get together in front of the fireplace again soon.

Wishing you warmth and cheer, dear Evangeline.

Love,
Hroshi

Dear Hroshi

Your latest joy-giving letter arrived on Friday. Like you, I'm not concerned about ever running out of joy-givers.

We might not be able to change the circumstances of our lives, but we can change the eyes through which we view them: a perfect lesson for me to be reminded of today. I had experienced a disappointment which caused my horn to lean forlornly over my forehead.

After reading your letter, it began to right itself once again. (Surely there is nothing quite as woeful as a unicorn with a toppled horn.)

Whenever I experience a horn-drooping day, I try to see it from a different perspective, and I remember that tomorrow brings a new day with fresh promise ...

the first day of the rest of my life!

Evangeline

Dear Hroshi

Yesterday's forlorn-horn event was a tonic: it reminded me to be ever thankful for *ordinary* days.

I don't know about you, Hroshi, but at times I get restless and long for more from life ... I ache for that missing piece that always seems to be just out of my reach.

The closer I get to it, the farther away it seems to move.

Yesterday restored my equilibrium.

When the ordinary is taken away, by illness, disappointment or bad news, it can serve to remind us of the joys of regular days.

There's much to be said about finding contentment in the rhythms of the ordinary.

Evangeline

Dear Evangeline

I, too, am restless on occasion.

But there is so much beauty all around us if we take the time to look for it, isn't there?

Hroshi

Dear Hroshi

Last night our power went out. I had been sound asleep but the deafening darkness woke me up.

At first I couldn't see, and my room was intimidating and unfamiliar, but as my eyes adjusted, I could distinguish objects that had been indiscernible moments earlier.

More time passed and more came into view ... things that initially weren't visible.

In our everyday lives, there is much around us that has not yet come into our view. There it is, patiently waiting for our eyes to adjust.

Evangeline

P.S. What do you see, Hroshi?

Evangeline

I find your image of the dark room—*forgive me*—enlightening. At first the "darkness" of a new family and a new language and a new home—a whole new world for me—seemed intimidating and unfamiliar. Then my eyes (and purple ears) adjusted, and I was able to distinguish objects I hadn't known about earlier.

Yes: there are so many things around us waiting for our eyes (or our ears, or our hearts) to bring into focus.

As I travelled on a train for the first time, I saw scenes of mountainous splendour such as had existed only in my wildest hippo-dreams.

Briefly: we left the city of *Praha* (Prague), traversed the Czech Republic for three hours, crossed the Bohemian border into Germany, enjoyed beautiful Bavarian countryside, crossed into Austria, rode around an enchanting lake, and finally entered Switzerland: land of cuckoo clocks, cheese fondues, fine chocolate and breathtaking scenery.

The Alps were paradise for a small grey hippo on her first train trip! Finally, we disembarked at Zurich Station. All in all, a Big Day for a little traveller waiting for her eyes to adjust.

As each new scene of beauty came into focus, my heart nearly split out of its seams at so much grandeur.

Springtime in Europe—seen from a train window—is a view I'd love to share with you.

Hroshi

Hroshi

You *did* just share it with me. That's one of the things I enjoy about words: they can take you anywhere.

Have you ever ridden on a carousel at the fair? It is my favourite ride, as there is an assortment of colourful animals, including unicorns.

I climb aboard a shiny white unicorn and dream I am flying as the carousel whirls around and around and up and down.

Whether I am up or down I find life exhilarating.

Evangeline

P.S. Here's a chorus about carousels from a song by Joni Mitchell:

 "And the seasons they go round and round
And the painted ponies go up and down."[xxv]

My dear Evangeline

Thank you for the carousel chorus—you always surprise me with your creative tastes. My own literary palette is expanding because of you.

While reading a book that both hippos and unicorns would enjoy,[xxvi] I thought of these additions to the topic under discussion:

Creativity is high on my joy-list. Pottery-makers and glass-blowers have earned my admiration, as have wordsmiths, silversmiths and blacksmiths. It never ceases to amaze me how an earthy clump of clay—or a dull chunk of rock, or block of glass, or wood, or steel—can yield such intricate results in the hands of a skilled artisan.

Literature. Is there anything that can take the place of a good book? Whether the writer is an old favourite, or a new find, few joys compare. Dusty, second-hand bookstores appeal to all my hippo-senses. I enjoy reading; being read to; writing; being written to—and I truly appreciate the literary accomplishments of a host of talented authors and artists.

Poetry brings me immeasurable joy.

Once in a while, I spend a Thursday evening reading with my human companions from a random selection of anthologies. We call ourselves the *No Inklings*—in fond memory of C. S. Lewis and like-minded souls who called their group the *Inklings*—and we each pick a favourite poem or poet to share. Perhaps I'll compile a personal anthology to send to you someday.

With my hippo-nose in a book,
Hroshi

Dear Hroshi

Prior to the start of our correspondence, I had *no inkling* of your fondness for poetry!

I admire your love of creative beauty and the way you express feelings with words so skilfully.

Here is a verse from a song that contains some beautiful words. The melody and instrumentation that accompany it are warm and wistful:

> Pussy willows,
> cattails,
> soft winds and roses.
> Rainbows in the woodland,
> water to my knee.
> Shivering,
> quivering,
> the warm breath of spring.
> Pussy willows,
> cattails,
> soft winds and roses.
>
> ~ Gordon Lightfoot[xxvii]

Hroshi, with your soft-grey coat, you fondly remind me of an extra-*extra* large pussy willow.

In your last letter you mentioned that poetry brings you joy. With that in mind, I have tried to express my joy-givers in poetic form for you:

I LOVE

The ocean.
Waves.
Sand.
Shells in my hand.
Smooth stones in my pocket.
A silvery locket.
A picture framed.
A whispered name.

Butterflies.
Dragonflies.
Fireflies.
Summer skies.

Pink cotton candy.
Merry-go-rounds.
Carnival sounds.

Horses
running in the rain.
The stark
jagged
trail from a jet plane.

The first soft
crocus
I spy.

Pussy willows.
Cattails.
Soft winds.
Rainbows.
Spring showers.
Fragrant flowers.

Hours
and
hours
of good books
in cozy nooks.

Choirs
singing.
Bells ringing.
Stained glass glistening.
Heaven stooping,
smiling,
listening.

Snow flakes.
Snowmen.
Scarves, earmuffs,
mittens
soft as kittens.

Candle light.
Star light.
Moonlight.
Geese in flight.

Downy pillows.
Scented sheets.
Cookies.
Cocoa and marshmallows.
Night-time treats.

Someone dear,
breathing softly,
lying near.

~ Evangeline Joy

Oh, Evangeline! I am at a loss for words.

My breath catches in my throat as I re-read the images on the page before me: your poem is simply beautiful. Thank you for sharing it with me. With your permission I'll read it aloud when our poetry group meets again on Thursday night.

In awe,
Hroshi

P.S. Evangeline, I see your hoofprints on every line, in every image. You are fully alive to the world around you. Perhaps that's the secret to writing a poem.

Dear Hroshi

I want to be able to see and appreciate the messages hidden in the most ordinary, everyday things, for it is often in the small things that the most valuable treasures can be found ...

... like a dewdrop on a blade of grass,
a determined green shoot pushing through the sidewalk,
or the last brown leaf clinging to a branch.

There is wonder to behold in the simplicity of a single snowflake glittering on the backdrop of a woollen mitten, or in the sharp contrast between a thorny stem and the exquisite velvet rose it supports.

The smallest things can inspire and give joy; they can be salubrious, like a smile, a gentle touch, an encouraging word, or ...

... a coloured envelope bearing bright words and thoughts, such as those you send to me.

The list goes on and on.

Mother Teresa understood this when she wrote:

"We can do no great things;
only small things with great love."[xxviii]

Evangeline

P.S. Salubrious means *promoting good health*: "wholesome for body, mind and soul."[xxix]

The unicorn wrote of small things and the hippo began to reflect.

Evangeline, dear

Upon further reflection, many of the small things are not so small after all, are they? Imagine a tiny pearl in an oyster shell.

I am intrigued by nuances and details. Reading something new that has been written in a fresh and captivating manner thrills me. Reading something well known and much loved for the umpteenth time also brings me pleasure.

I am currently memorising your lovely poem, Evangeline Joy. Its small treasures delight me each time I recite the words. Possibly because it's midwinter, the images close to my heart today are contained in the lines:

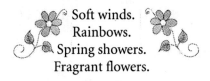

Soft winds.
Rainbows.
Spring showers.
Fragrant flowers.

In one brief verse you captured (for me) the sound of the wind, rustling through the remaining leaves of autumn; the burst of brilliant colour in a rain-grey sky; the gentle warmth of spring moisture soaking into dry fields; and the sudden unexpected scent of jasmine and rose petals.

Another favourite mental photograph is the one of horses running in the rain. Years ago I watched two horses galloping on a nearby farm. They appeared wild and free, abandoning themselves to the joy of the moment. Despite the cloudy prairie skies, the day was brighter because of their vitality. Your poem brought them to mind and I smiled at the memory, long forgotten.

Hroshi

As the unicorn carefully re-read her friend's response to her poem, she marvelled anew at the latent power of words.

Words,
she reflected,
were like seeds,
and one never quite knew
what might grow from them.
The thought stirred her
with a desire
to plant gardens
and gardens
of words.

Closing her eyes,
she dreamily imagined
words of every
size,
shape
and colour,
dancing in a row.

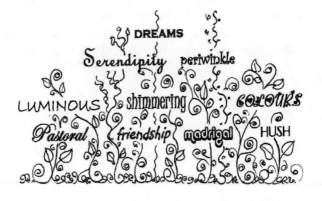

Dear Hroshi

Sometime we must go for a walk in the rain together. I know how much you enjoy water! I will have to wear a raincoat, because my fur is not waterproof like yours, and it gets terribly matted when wet.

It was fun to talk on the phone this morning and find out that both of us are feeling refreshed by the rainfall. Your love of rain has had a positive influence on me.

I walked and walked this morning ... getting soaking wet and not minding it one little bit. It's only water, and water eventually dries.

Beads of rain trickled down my unicorn horn and clung to my eyelashes, like fat happy tears. It was easy to forget about all the things that needed doing and to just enjoy *being*.

So let's go rain-walking soon, my friend.

If we spot a rainbow, we can both make a wish ...

"And the dreams that you dare to dream really do come true."xxx

What are your dreams, Hroshi?

Evangeline J

P.S. When we get home, we can each have a steaming mug of ginger tea.

The unicorn's final question: What are your dreams? *launched the dreamy hippo off into the space where dreams reside.*

I dream of being a travelling hippo, and of exploring the furthermost curves of creation.

I dream of returning to Prague, city of 100 spires, to retrace the hippo-steps of my childhood.

I dream of being a global correspondent and of writing to fellow letter-lovers.

I dream of seeing our kindred spirit correspondence in print.

I dream of encouraging others to dream.

I dream of heaven.

Do *you* dream, dear Evangeline Joy?

Hroshi

P.S. I appreciate dream-chasers (as opposed to dream-squashers). So many people in our world prevent us from dreaming—often without even knowing they're doing so. Don't *ever* let me rain on your dreams.

I want to listen; I want to share your joy; I want to dream with you!

(I also want to learn to paint and play the piano, though not simultaneously.)

Dear Hroshi

I believe that it is important to give voice to your dreams.

Reading your last letter inspired me to write a poem about you being a travelling hippo on an imaginary trip to Paris.

Don't you look exceedingly cosmopolitan, standing beside the Eiffel Tower? *I* think so, and I find you hugely photogenic. Have you attended finishing school somewhere?

When you read it, please pronounce Paris /"Pa *ree*"/ and Hroshi /"H*ro* she"/. (*Trés* French, don't you agree?)

HROSHI EN PARIS

While sightseeing in gay Paris
The Frenchmen took one look at me:
Ils ont dit,
"Who can that 'ippo be,
Arrayed in *couture*-finery?"
I sweetly smiled;
"*Alors,*" *j'ai dit* ...
"*C'est moi!*
Et je m'appelle
Hroshi."

Ton amie,
Evangeline

Hroshi en Paris made me blush with pleasure down to my exceedingly cosmopolitan toes! No one has ever written a poem about me in a foreign language before!

Merci beaucoup, mon amie merveilleuse!*

Thanks for saying you find me hugely photogenic—that would be how *I* would describe *you*, dear friend. And as for thinking I attended a finishing school? I laugh out loud in your direction!

Amitiés,
Hroshi
(*trés française, n'est-ce pas?*)**

Pas d'en Paris, malheureusement!***

P.S. Pardon my French!

**Merci beaucoup, mon amie merveilleuse!*
Thank you very much, my marvellous friend!

**Amitiés, Hroshi (*trés française, n'est-ce pas?*)
Affectionately, Hroshi (very French, not so?)

****Pas d'en Paris, malheureusement!*
Not in Paris, unfortunately!

Reading
about
the hippo's
stardust dreams
prompted the unicorn to start dreaming again.
She had once been a great believer in dreams,
but had experienced some of the dream-breakers
her friend mentioned.

As she quietly
pondered this,
it seemed
as though a cloud
of iridescent-winged
dragonflies
began to soar
inside of her.

Could it be that her dreams were taking flight again?

Dear Hroshi

Already one of your dreams has come true: you have encouraged me to dream again ...

Recently you wrote: *Each tiny feather of frozen glass has its very own fingerprint.* All of us leave our fingerprints upon this world ... some in positive ways and others in not-so-positive ways.

One of my dreams is to leave my hoofprints in this world in a loving way.

Evangeline Joy

P.S. "The whole universe is but the footprint of divine goodness."[xxxi]

Dear Reader,

What are your dreams?

....
....
....
....
....
....
....
....
....
....
....
....
....

Evangeline and Hroshi

Dear Hroshi

The photo you sent of us dreaming together in front of the fire-place during our recent visit made me smile. What a treasured memento of our time together.

The marshmallows we roasted were sublime ... sticky and sweet and worth the time it took us to toast them to a perfect golden brown.

Love,
Evangeline

Dear Evangeline

How would you feel if I described you as my muse?

The noun **muse** comes from Greek and Roman mythology, and refers to the goddesses who preside over branches of learning and the arts, while the verb means *to ponder*.

I'm thinking you're my muse in the verb-sense: you cause me to stop and ponder the important aspects of life, such as small things, joy-givers and dreams.

Your gift with words is like a silver spoon that stirs up my inner being, inspiring me and piquing my curiosity about the mysteries and marvels of life.

Hroshi

The unicorn was touched by her friend's affirmation.

Small things.
Joy-givers.
Dreams.

At first glance, they could appear insignificant, but they were like a matchstick to someone gazing at an unlit candle.

Dear Hroshi

I am touched that you would think of me as a muse. (Or was that *amuse*?)

Taking out my big dictionary I found the following definitions for muse:

to stand with muzzle in the air
and
to wonder or marvel; to dream.

You may call me a muse if I may call you a **mystic**: *one who intuitively comprehends truths beyond human understanding.*

Evangeline

Dear Evangeline Joy

(Sigh.) Thank you for your encouraging (and a-musing) letter. It arrived on a bottom-of-the-lake day. (Even river-dwellers have those.)

I stopped wallowing in the mire—and rolling in the river grass—just long enough to read your kind words. While your muzzle was raised, my hippo-heart was heavy.

My friend, I shall try to see the mystical qualities that you see in me.

However, I have a recurring dream on occasion that makes me wonder: I find myself in a department store in Prague, surrounded by dozens of other Hroshi-hippos, just like me.

They, too, are soft and grey, with purple paws and ears. One by one they are pulled off the shelves and placed in shopping baskets and trolleys—and then I awake, restless. I don't know what my dream means, but I do know that I find no comfort in it.

Once upon a time I was told that I was merely a stuffed toy. Perhaps I really am filled with sawdust or beans.

Are we unique? Or are there others just like us?

Hroshi

Dear friend beyond compare

If it is any consolation to you, I suspect that all of us have moments when we question our individuality.

Outwardly all of us share similarities to those of our kind, but no, Hroshi, in this whole big blue world, there is no one just like you or me.

Have you ever cut open a Christmas pudding and looked inside? Each one is russet and round, practically impossible to tell apart. Inside, however, there is a profusion of:

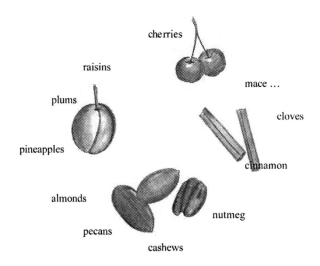

cherries

raisins

mace ...

plums

cloves

pineapples

cinnamon

almonds

nutmeg

pecans

cashews

... a measured and deliberate conglomeration of multi-coloured and flavourful ingredients, making each savoury dessert unlike any other. No pudding has the same ingredients in precisely the same proportion as another.

Like this festive dessert, your inner being is one-of-a-kind.

Evangeline

Dear Evangeline

Today I can only say a simple thank you for your last letter. I hope to find a way to express how I feel.

Love,
Hroshi

P.S. Sometimes when I find myself at a loss for words, fragments of poetry drift across the windswept spaces of my mind. Into the dryness flows the oasis of our friendship.

Each thought that appears on the empty sheet before me contains an image of you, and the phrases combine to form sentences and stanzas.

Please accept these two dozen lines as a gesture of gratitude for your inspiring correspondence:

ODE TO EVANGELINE THE UNICORN

Galloping hoofbeats on a seaweed-strewn beach;
You're a field of white daisies with centres of gold.
Willing to learn, yet with so much to teach;
Wise and youthful you are, with a soul that is old …

After a drought, you are earth's gentle rain;
Bright light of the sun after wrath of the storm.
Healing you bring, in the midst of the pain;
When winter descends, your friendship stays warm …

You're the madrigal's call, unexpected and rare;
A splash of green moss in a forest of browns.
You are ready to comfort: I turn, and you're there;
A party for children—with presents and clowns …

You're Jerry Spinelli's *Stargirl*—a treat—
And Elizabeth Goudge's *Little White Horse*.
You're a rainbow of crayons, fruit-scented and sweet;
A cloudburst of stardust, aquarian force …

Prisms dance on your unique horn, blue as the sky;
Your dazz'ling white fur carries traces of snow.
You're the scent of vanilla baked in crisp apple pie
And the warmth of a log fire at thirty below …

Evangeline, dear, on this bright snowy eve,
I thank our Creator for the gift that He's giv'n;
I treasure the dreams that *you* make me believe
And I praise God above for my own friend from heav'n!

~ Hroshi the hippo (your kindred spirit)

Dear Hroshi

The words of your ode filled me with wonder and gratitude. They were a sparkling window through which I gazed to gain a clearer vision of myself as well as a glimpse into your bountiful hippo-heart.

Sometimes it is hard to see ourselves clearly ... our viewpoint is simply too close. It takes a good friend like you to bring the picture into focus.

Morning has not yet broken as I sit here in the quiet. I turn my gaze expectantly towards the window and raise my muzzle to the night sky.

The stars smile down from the heavens, and I ponder the depths of the infinite.

Although it is a wintry night, I feel snug and cozy.

As this season draws to a close, I fondly recall the cheery envelopes that have winged their way between us: so many letters in so short a time.

Like an arrow, a star arches across the sky and I make a wish upon it. How wonderful it would be to compile our hippo and unicorn letters into an anthology.

At such a thought, these words burst within me like fireworks:

at night
when the moon
is a blinking eye
and the stars
scatter stardust
o'er a windswept sky,
i dance with you.

we dance
through the night
you and i
and the moon
and the stars
in the sky
dance, too.

Dreamily dancing,
Evangeline

Dear Evangeline

yes, under the moon
with its welcoming eye
while the stars scatter stardust
we dance: you and i

while the moon and the stars
in the sky dance, too
you and i—kindred souls—
dance for joy: me and you

and the rainbows of colour
and comets of fire
and cloudbursts of heaven
take us dancing up higher

yes, under the stars
with their twinkling glow
we dance ever upwards:
up ... up ... UP we go!

Starry-eyed,
Hroshi

EPILOGUE

And now,
dear Reader,
as together we close
the flap
of the last envelope,
you are invited
to lift your gaze
skyward.

If the lighting is right,
you might glimpse
Hroshi and Evangeline
dancing in the moonlight ...

... dancing and dreaming.

And the dreams that we dare to dream really do come true.

AFTERWORD

Dear Reader

Hroshi and Evangeline are still writing, and we invite you to take a peek inside an envelope or two from their next anthology.

Here's an excerpt from *The Pocket Book*.

POCKETS

There are all kinds of pockets around us
if we have the eyes to see.
A mug's a container for cocoa;
a teacup pockets sweet tea.

An acorn's a pocket for oak trees,
and a nest is a pocket for birds.
A mailbag's a pocket for letters
and a book is a pocket for words.

A locket's a pocket for faces
of family or friends we hold dear.
A heart is a pocket of feelings
for loved ones distant or near.

And now that we've got you started,
why don't you think of some too?
There are pockets right under our noses:
look around and you'll see that it's true!

 Evangeline and Hroshi

Dear Hroshi

This morning, stopping to watch a small fuzzy caterpillar inching her way across a branch, I thought (briefly) about putting her in my pocket.

Thankfully reason prevailed!

Seeing her measured, steady progress made me think how wise it is to take life an inch at a time ... to be purposeful and persistent in the journey and enjoy the view.

That's my pocket thought for today. What's yours?

Evangeline

Dear Evangeline

How I needed to read your wise words today. Has somebody fast-forwarded my life? I feel torn in several directions this week. Soon my African grandmother will need to re-stitch my seams yet again!

The image of the unhurried caterpillar calmed my hippo-heart.

Today I shall s-l-o-w down and enjoy the journey, appreciating today's pockets of time, minute by minute.

Hroshi

Dear Reader

We hope that you have enjoyed *The Hippo and the Unicorn: A Rainbow of Words.*

We would be delighted to read your responses.

We have a penchant for old-fashioned envelope-and-stamp mail, and would be over the moon to hear from you.

Write to us c/o:

gem*n*i designs inc.
P. O. Box 8001
Cochrane RPO
305–1ˢᵗ Street
Cochrane, AB
T4C 2J7
Canada

We look forward to your letters,

Elaine and Lindsie,
Hroshi and Evangeline Joy

You could also write to us via e-mail at:

haxtonphillips@gmail.com

or at our company address:

gem.n.idesigns@gmail.com

FOOTNOTES

i   *The Cataract of Lodore, by Robert Southey* (1774–1843).

ii   Madeleine L'Engle (1918–2007).

iii   Henry Wadsworth Longfellow (1807–1882).

iv   "Mistress of the Margin" is a phrase of unknown origin, possibly attributed to the Desert Mothers.

v   *On Marriage*, by Kahlil Gibran (1883–1931).

vi   *Recipe for a Hippopotamus Sandwich*, by Shel Silverstein (1932–1999).

vii   *I Wandered Lonely as a Cloud* (or *The Daffodils*), by William Wordsworth (1770–1850).

viii   Henry James (1843–1916).

ix   *Synesthesia*, by Heather Blush (http://www.heatherblush.com).

x   *Charlotte's Web*, by E. B. White (1899–1985).

xi   Gloria the unicorn lives in California with Christina Stephenson.

xii   Gilbert White (1720–1793).

xiii   Vincent van Gogh (1853–1890).

xiv   *Coffee With Warren*, by Warren Harbeck, in the *Cochrane Eagle*, 26 Nov and 3 Dec 2003 (JoinMe@coffeewithwarren.com).

xv   Christine Kupchenko Dubetz.

xvi   *The Ballad of Beautiful Words*, by John McCutcheon (1870–1949).

xvii   Camelot the bear lives with the Carr family in Coventry.

xviii   *I Had A Hippopotamus*, by Patrick Barrington (1908–1990).

xix   *The Unicorn*, by Shel Silverstein (1932–1999).

xx   *Through the Looking-Glass*, by Lewis Carroll (1832–1898).

xxi   "*This Is the Creature*," by Rainer Maria Rilke (1875–1926).

xxii   *Animal Crackers*, by Christopher Morley (1890–1957).

xxiii   "Who is like the LORD our God, the One who sits enthroned on high, who stoops down to look on the heavens and the earth?" (Psalm 113:5-6, NIV).

xxiv   "Life is what we are alive to. It is not length but breadth ... Be alive to ... goodness, kindness, purity, love, history, poetry, music, flowers, stars, God, and eternal hope." Maltbie D. Babcock (1858–1901).

xxv   *The Circle Game*, by Joni Mitchell (1943–).

xxvi   *Kingfisher Days*, by Susan Coyne (2002).

xxvii   *Pussy Willows, Cattails*, by Gordon Lightfoot (1938–).

xxviii Mother Teresa (1910–1997).

xxix   *The Positive Dictionary*, by Dr. Phil Minnaar (http://www.thepositivedictionary.com).

xxx   *Over the Rainbow*, by E. Y. "Yip" Harburg (1896–1981).

xxxi   Dante Alighieri (1265–1321).

978-0-595-43670-5
0-595-43670-6

Printed in the United States
95336LV00005B/280-441/A

9 780595 436705